For Ella
with love from Niki.

Copyright © 2001 by Niki Daly
First published in Great Britain by Bloomsbury Children's Books, 2001
Printed in Hong Kong by Wing King Tong
First American edition, 2002
1   3   5   7   9   10   8   6   4   2

Library of Congress Cataloging-in-Publication Data
Daly, Niki.
  Old Bob's brown bear / story and pictures by Niki Daly.— 1st Amer. ed.
    p.   cm.
  Summary: Old Bob gets a teddy bear for his birthday because he never had one as a child,
but his granddaughter, thinking the bear deserves better than to be stuck between dusty books,
wants to take him home.
  ISBN 0-374-35612-2
  [1. Teddy bears—Fiction.   2. Toys—Fiction.   3. Grandfathers—Fiction.   4. Grandparent and child—Fiction.]
I. Title.

PZ7.D1715 Ol 2002
[E]—dc21

2001040948

Old Bob's Brown Bear

Story and Pictures by Niki Daly

FARRAR STRAUS GIROUX • NEW YORK

On Old Bob's birthday, Gran gave him a teddy bear.

"But old men don't play with teddy bears," said Emma, watching her grandpa unwrap his present.

"Well, Old Bob always said he wanted a teddy bear," said Gran.

"Why?" asked Emma.

"Because I never had one when I was a little boy," explained Old Bob.

Old Bob looked at Teddy. Teddy looked at Old Bob. Something was wrong.

"It's very nicely made," said Old Bob.

Old Bob kept saying nice things about his teddy bear. But Emma could tell . . .

Old Bob didn't LOVE his brown bear.

When they had tea and birthday cake, Old Bob squeezed Teddy between his dusty books. Emma got Teddy down and hugged him.

She sat on the floor and fed Teddy some of Old Bob's birthday cake.

When it was time to go, Emma held Teddy very close to her. Mom said, "You must put Teddy down now, Emma. It's time to go home."

But Emma held Teddy even closer and cried,
"I want Teddy!"

"You can play with Teddy the next time you visit," said Gran.
Emma gave Teddy back to Old Bob, but she wasn't happy.
She saw how Old Bob pushed Teddy back between his dusty
old books.

The next time Emma visited Old Bob, she found Teddy between the same dusty books in the dark study.

"Teddy's been waiting for you, Emma," said Old Bob.

Emma squeezed Teddy. Teddy was starting to smell like Old Bob's dusty books.

Emma and Teddy looked at Old Bob's books.
Emma liked the one filled with photographs. So Old
Bob showed Emma a photograph of a little boy.

"That's me with the wind-up train I got for
my birthday when I was your age," said Old Bob.

"But you didn't have a teddy," sighed Emma.

"No," said Old Bob, "and I've always wanted
one of those old fuzzy-wuzzy teddy bears that
are all worn out with lots and lots of love."

Emma gave Old Bob's new teddy a cuddle.

When it was time to go home, Mom said, "Give Teddy back to Old Bob, Emma."

"Teddy will be here next time you visit," said Gran.

But Emma clutched Teddy so tightly that Mom had to tug on Teddy's legs. Still Emma hung on and wailed.

"I want Teddy!"

"Maybe Teddy can have a vacation with you," said Old
Bob. "And you can bring him back next time you visit us."
Old Bob gave Emma his scarf as a blanket for Teddy.

Teddy had a lovely vacation with Emma. They had a picnic in the garden with Emma's other toys. They went shopping.

They went to the beach and got wet and full
of sunscreen and sand.

When they got home, Emma gave Teddy a
bubble bath.

After his bath,
Emma hung him
up to dry.

When he was dry,
she gave his ears
a good brush.

Mom found one of Emma's old baby shirts for Teddy.
At bedtime, Emma snuggled up against him. He didn't smell like Old Bob's books anymore.

When Old Bob saw Teddy again, he chuckled. "Teddy must have had a lovely vacation—just look at him!"

Emma told Old Bob all about Teddy's vacation.

But when it was time to go home, Mom said, "Give Teddy back to Old Bob now, Emma. When we visit, you can play with him again."

But Emma held on to Teddy and cried,

"I want Teddy!"

"Let's ask Old Bob what he thinks,"
said Gran.
    Old Bob looked at Teddy.
    Emma looked at Old Bob.
It looked as though he was
beginning to love Teddy.
    But Old Bob said,
"Well, perhaps Emma
can go on looking
after Teddy for me."

When Old Bob waved goodbye, he called,
"Come back soon and don't
forget to bring Teddy!"

Emma looked after Teddy for a long, long time. She loved
him so much that the fur around his nose and tummy got
hugged right off.

When he got all tangled up, Emma brushed the fur on his ears until he looked like a fuzzy-wuzzy teddy bear.

Later, when Emma started school, she didn't see Old Bob quite so often. Old Bob didn't see Teddy for a very long time.

Then, during one school vacation, Old Bob visited
Emma and noticed that Teddy was no longer on
Emma's bed.

"Where's Teddy?" asked Old Bob.

"Oh, he's in my toy box with my old toys," said
Emma.

Old Bob scratched around among Emma's toys.
At the bottom, he found Teddy, lying tangled up in
an old baby shirt.

Old Bob smiled.

"What an old bear you've become," said Old Bob, patting Teddy's worn-out tummy.

Emma stopped brushing her doll's long blond silky hair and smiled at Old Bob.

"He's a fuzzy-wuzzy old teddy bear now," said Emma.

Old Bob looked at Teddy.

And Teddy looked at Old Bob.

"I want Teddy!" said Old Bob suddenly.

When Emma saw the happy look on Old Bob's face, she smiled and said, "That's okay, Old Bob, you can have Teddy. He's a very old bear now."

Old Bob hugged Teddy.

What was that smell?

Old Bob could smell cookies and sticky fingers. He could smell sweet grass and fruit juice. He could smell salty sea and sunscreen. He could smell squeaky toys and bubble bath. He closed his eyes and smiled.

Yes, Old Bob could smell lots
and lots of . . .
love!